VISION

SEEING IS ACHIEVING

ALLAN SEALY

LIFE AND SUCCESS PUBLISHING
www.abookinsideyou.com

Life and Success Media Ltd
email info@abookinsideyou.com
www.abookinsideyou.com

ISBN: 978-1-907402-86-9

Cover design & layout by
miadesign.com

TABLE OF CONTENTS

Dedication   5

Introduction   7

PART ONE   What Is Man?   **15**

Chapter 1   The Three Heavens   21

Chapter 2   The Three Dimensions of Man   33

Chapter 3   The Origin of Things   41

Chapter 4   The Significance of Vision   47

Chapter 5   Mankind Defined   57

PART TWO   Manifesting Your Vision   **67**

Chapter 6   Faith in Your Vision   69

Chapter 7   Don't Look Up, Look within   75

Chapter 8   Recognize What You Have   83

Chapter 9   Get Wisdom   91

Chapter 10   Dare To Dream Big   99

Chapter 11   Use Time Well   105

Chapter 12   Start from the End   115

PART THREE   The Power of Vision   123

Chapter 13   See, Believe, Take Action
             and Receive   125

Chapter 14   Be Inspired   131

Chapter 15   The Divine Power of Vision   137

Dedication

This Book is dedicated to
my daughters, Jasmin & Jada.
I love you both deeply.

Special Thanks

I want to give special thanks to:

My Father (The Wise One)
- for your wisdom, love and guidance -

My Mother (My Rock)
- for your unfailing love and sacrifice -

Bishop Dr. Wayne Malcolm
(The Business Pastor)
- thank you for your vision -

LET THERE BE LIGHT

It's been almost 25 years since I made the decision to follow my passion for art. This decision was made, having just completed 7 years of arduous study in electronics, culminating in a degree in Electronic engineering. Why spend so many years studying electronics, only to embark in a career in art? Well to begin with, I have always been passionate about art, and spent much of my childhood drawing and painting. I had every intention of becoming an artist by profession. Unfortunately, a schoolteacher told me that I would not be able to make a good living from art, regardless of my talent. This news was devastating to me, especially coming from my art teacher! I have always been very ambitious, so the thought of struggling to make money from art did not rest well with me.

As an alternative, I decided to pursue a career in electronics. It was a subject I found interesting and it seemed to be a more stable profession. By the time I started attending University, having completed the necessary college courses, the UK was experiencing a recession. This prevented me, and many other students, from attaining the 12 months work experience that was integral to the course. As a result, I obtained my degree, forgoing the crucial work experience that would have endowed me with valuable practical skills. To this day, I couldn't fix a kettle if my life depended on it! Undeterred, I went into the big wide world determined to get a job in electronics and start my meteoric climb to the top (whatever that was). After a year of receiving rejection letters, anxiety and disappointment had all but eaten away my optimism.

Then I decided to take up art again (after a 7 year hiatus), more for therapeutic reasons than anything else. I dusted off the unfinished drawings I had started way back when, and got to work. It did not take long for that overwhelming and somewhat addictive enthusiasm for art to return. Hours of drawing replaced looking for a job, a luxury I could well afford, as I was still living under my mother's roof.

My mother's home was a hub for many of her fellow church members, eager to taste her renowned Bajan cuisines! As a result of these many 'intrusions' to my home, my artwork soon came to the attention of the senior pastor. I must have made an impression, as I was asked by one of the church deacons to design a flier for an upcoming event. Soon after, other pastors sought my handiwork, which I gladly did it (for next to nothing), as I relished the novelty of someone wanting me to design for them. It was then that I began to explore the possibility of actually becoming a freelance graphic designer. At the same time, under the guidance of my cousin (who had a relatively lucrative career as an electrical engineer), significant steps had been made to set me up as a telecommunications engineer. It was at this juncture that I was faced with the dilemma of what path I should take. My passion and gift was art, however, I was reluctant to turn my back on electronics after so many years of study. I was stuck at a crossroad, looking for answers.

The answer came a year later when I attended a seminar held by a Bahamian Pastor named Dr. Myles Munroe, who at that time (early 90's) was relatively unknown in the UK. He was speaking about 'releasing your potential' and it was in one of his breakout sessions that I heard these life changing words:

*"Your gifts and talents were given to you
for a divine purpose"*

Those words blew my young mind on many levels. First of all, the concept of a divine purpose for my life was completely foreign to me. Did I lack ambition? Certainly not! However, the idea of 'God' having a plan and purpose for my life was not something I had ever considered. Added to that, as my only obvious gift at the time was art, I could not see how or why a hobby, that at best could be used to earn a living, should play any part in some divine plan and purpose. That in itself implied that my talent was more than just my own personal interest, it was something *given* to me *on purpose*, for a purpose. That day, I experienced a paradigm shift and began to see things from a totally different perspective. If God indeed had a purpose for my life, then to do anything else would be meaningless! From then on, I became 'purpose driven,' and 'vision oriented.' I began to see the importance of following one's passion, as it emanates from one's purpose and destiny. When I left that meeting my dilemma had vanished; I would follow the path that art was leading me to. That path has led me to a career that was beyond what I could see at the time - from fashion design to owning a sought after graphic design company, expanding into magazine publishing, book publishing, and marketing. I am also an author, life coach, actor, motivational speaker, and event organizer.

Though labeled as 'painfully shy' in my early 20's, I now run a success media company and speak to various groups and audiences internationally. I've been interviewed multiple times on radio and TV, and have also acted in film and theater. All of this came about from my decision to follow my passion – and the best is yet to come!

However, when I say that I have had a career that I could not presently see, that is not exactly true. I saw it in my daydreams, but did not know at the time that daydreams are real. I saw it whenever I saw Pastor Dennis Scotland give one of his inspirational, down-to-earth, humorous, and thought provoking sermons. My vision has presented itself with every turn, getting clearer through good times, and even clearer through the bad times. Ever since my eyes we opened on the day of that life-changing seminar, my vision has been my constant companion.

Walking in the light

One other thing I learnt that day, was the biblical concept of light and darkness. Simply put, knowledge is light and ignorance is darkness. Ignorance blinds us from the truth about ourselves and also prevents us from seeing solutions and recognizing opportunities. The inability to see, lies at the root of the worlds problems. But as quickly as darkness disappears when light is shone, problems will also vanish when knowledge shines bright.

The true power of light is not measured in how brightly it shines, but in it's ability to allow you to see through *barriers*. Imagine being in a windowless room with the lights turned off, leaving you in complete darkness. Imagine the light for that room being controlled by a dimmer switch. If you only turn the switch slightly, the light will come on, but not enough to give you a full view of the room. As a result, the room will be dim and there will be parts or details of the room that you cannot see. Even the color of the wall may not be discernible. As you turn the switch more, the room becomes brighter and you will be able to see more of the room. When you turn the switch on fully, you will be able to see the room in its entirety - the door, the ceiling, and all the contents of the room. You will be able to see if the room is tidy or disorganized, whether it's in good condition or in need of repair. Basically you will be able to see the appearance of your surroundings. What you won't be able to see, however, is what lies beyond the walls of the room. This is because the walls are opaque, making it inpenitratable to white light. Even if a floodlight were shone in that room you still would not be able to see beyond the walls.

There are many people who are walking around in darkness, void of a compelling vision for their lives. There are many still, living a dissatisfied and unfulfillled life. As life goes on, they become more and more aware of the true condition of their lives, and the need for change. But that awareness does not allow them to see beyond the limitations of their environment, their jobs, their circumstances, their paradigm, or even that of time.

That is why each of us needs to have vision. Not the vision that is seen through our eyes, but that which is revealed in our hearts. The vision of your heart will enable you see pass the limitations of time, revealing to you a future that only you can create. The vision of your heart will reveal your true potential and power. The vision of your heart will elevate your mind and expand your thinking so that you would truly believe that all things are possible. We were all created on purpose for a purpose. Your parents cannot assign purpose to you. You must discover it for yourself. However, the clues to your purpose are not hard to find. They are hidden in plain sight! It is only for you to recognize that what you see in your heart is not a pipe dream, but a window into your future, and a revelation of your purpose. This book was written to help you realize your purpose and your destiny, by enabling you to:

- understand who you really are,
- discover your passion
- understand the significance of your vision
- discover your creative power
- manifest your vision
- and unleash your awesome potential.

This book will inspire you to believe in your dreams and *hang-out* in your future. Your future lies within you. See beyond the limitations of your circumstances and dare to dream big.

Your vision awaits your action!

VISION

PART ONE

WHAT IS MAN?

INTRO

When I look at your heavens, the creation of your fingers, the moon and the stars that you have set in place, what is man that you remember him or the Son of Man that you take care of him? You have made him a little lower than yourself. You have crowned him with glory and honor. You have made him rule what your hands created. You have put everything under his control.

(Psalms 8:3-6 GWT)

Amidst the awesome wonders of creation, man stands at the very peak. Looking at our physicality, you may strongly disagree with my assertion. After all, our bodies are weak and tender, and our physical strength is no match to many of the creatures that roam our planet. However, our physical frame is only an incarnation of who we really are.

According to Psalms 8, we were originally made a little lower than God Himself! Although many Bible translations use the word 'angels' instead of God, one only has to look up the word used in the original Hebrew language to see that the word 'Elohiym' is used. Elohiym is the plural word used to denote God in His fullness; Father, Son, and Holy Spirit. In the original text, it is the Hebrew word used in the book of Genesis, identifying God in all His creative acts. Here are some examples below:

In the beginning Elohiym created the heaven and the earth. (Genesis 1:1)

And the Spirit of Elohiym moved upon the face of the waters. (Genesis 1:2)

And Elohiym said, Let there be light: and there was light. (Genesis 1:3)

And Elohiym saw the light, that it was good: and Elohiym divided the light from the darkness. (Genesis 1:4)

And Elohiym called the light Day, and the darkness he called Night. (Genesis 1:5)

So, man indeed was made a little lower than God, making him higher than the angels! Despite the fact that Angels are stronger and arguably more impressive, their value and their rank fall short in the eyes of God. Angels fell and rebelled long before man did. However, where a redemptive plan of salvation (through Christ) was set in place for mankind, only Hell awaits the fallen angels. Man was given dominion over the works of God's hands, whereas angels were assigned to be ministering servants to man.

So what is man that makes him so valuable to God? Clearly, we are more than what we see in the mirror. But why would He sacrifice everything for us? Is it only because we are His children, or is there something else that makes us so valuable? To answer this question, we must delve into the field of spiritual science. Similar to metaphysics, spiritual science is the study of first principles. With the aid of spiritual sciences, we unveil the true origin of things, which in turn enables us to comprehend the true nature of the universe.

The words 'spiritual' and 'science' may appear mutually exclusive when joined together, in light of the many scientists who refute the very existence of God. Spiritual science may also seem like an oxymoron to many religious people. However, there is a science behind everything God does. There is a science to spiritual things as well as a science to physical things. There is a science to the mind, spirit, and body.

So in our quest to understand what is man, let us see what spiritual science reveals about the universe and its make up.

VISION

Chapter 1

THE THREE HEAVENS

*In the beginning, God created the heavens
and the Earth...*

In the Bible, the universe is described as the Heavens and the Earth. This description depicts the universe as being both physical and spiritual. The physical world is the world you can see, rooted in a spiritual world that you cannot see. When we look at a plant, we know there is more to it than what we can see, in that its roots are hidden in the earth. This is a simplified analogy of the relationship between the spiritual and natural realms: the seen coexisting with the unseen. However, the universe is more complex than this depiction.

"I know a man in Christ who fourteen years ago whether in the body I do not know, or whether out of the body I do not know, God knows such a one was caught up to the third heaven. And I know such a man - whether in the body or out of the body I do not know, God knows how he was caught up into Paradise and heard inexpressible words, which it is not lawful for a man to utter." (2 Corinthians 12:2-4)

Paul's dramatic recount of being caught up to 'Paradise' gives us key insight into the true nature of the universe. According to Paul, Paradise is the third heaven. If Paradise is the third heaven, then there must also be a first and a second heaven. The heavens can also be described as realms, realities or worlds. The existence of multiple worlds is supported by the Bible's assertion that,

"By faith we understand that the worlds were framed by the word of God, so that the things which are seen were not made of things which are visible." (Heb:11v3)

Coupled together with Paul's experience we come to the understanding that the universe consists of 3 heavens, 3 worlds, 3 realms, and 3 realities.

The First Heaven

The creation of the first heaven is described in Genesis where God created a firmament and separated the waters from the earth from that of the firmament. He called the firmament 'heaven,' which symbolizes the boundary of the physical natural realm. The physical realm is where spiritual things are manifested into their physical counterpart. As a result, this is the realm of physical reality.

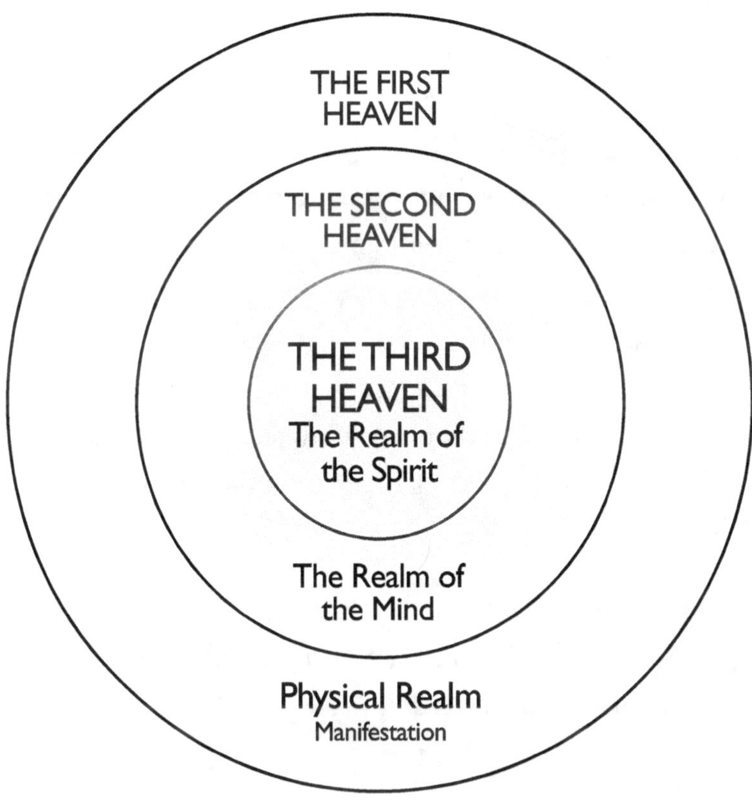

The true make-up of the universe

The Second Heaven

The second heaven is the realm of mind, thought, and imagination. It can also be termed as the realm of human achievement. This vast and multidimensional realm is formed by the collective conscious and imaginations of mankind. It must be understood that the mind space is a 'real space,' just as your city or your country is a real space. The realm of the mind is a greater reality than physical reality. It is the 'space' and dimension of our universe from which mental laws operate. Much has been written about mental laws and the ability to achieve success because of them. Mental laws are higher than physical laws in that they supersede all physical limitations. By applying them, you can achieve whatever you put your mind to, and are only limited by the limitations you impose on yourself. Here are some examples of mental laws:

The Law of Attraction

You are a living magnet and attract whatever is in alignment with your dominant thoughts.

The Law of Cause and Effect

For every effect in your life, there is a definite or specific cause.

The Law of Expectations

Whatever you expect with confidence becomes your self-fulfillling prophecy.

The Law of Correspondence

Your outer world corresponds to your inner world. You must *be*, rather than do!

The Law of Creativity

All positive change and progress in your
life begin with new ideas.

The Law of Control

You feel good or positive about yourself to
the degree to which you are in control of
your own life.

The Law of Substitution

The conscious mind can hold only one thought at a time, positive or negative. You can replace a negative thought with a positive thought.

The Law of Indirect Effort

In our relationship with other people, we have a tendency to get what we want indirectly faster than directly.

The Law of Emotion

The stronger your desire to achieve a goal, the more quickly it will be achieved.

The Law of Forgiveness

You are mentally healthy to the degree to which you can forgive and forget grievances against you.

The cornerstone of all mental laws is the law of belief. Also dubbed, 'the law of human achievement,' this law states that:

'Reality is the product of what you believe.'

Each of us would like to think that what we see is a reality. However, the way we interpret the world is determined by a number of factors such as mental filters, mental fortitude, mental disposition, and beliefs. Where one sees limitations, another sees opportunity. Both are realities subject only to what you believe. For that reason, the realm of mind, thought, and imagination can also be deemed as the realm of personal reality. We live in a world that is not only subject to our own sense of reality, but also forged and shaped by the thoughts and personal reality of others. Thomas Edison saw a world illuminated by the incandescent light bulb rather than lanterns. Henry Ford's vision made it possible for us to be transported by machines instead of horses. Martin Luther King Jr's 'dream' of racial equality broke the back of racism in America. Steve Job's passion for technology clothed in beauty caused the whole world to fall head-over-heels in love with smartphones and tablets! These are just a few examples of how personal reality impacts and shapes our world. In essence, personal reality is the medium of man's creative power. Much of what is created or changed in our world came through the inner sanctum of personal reality.

The Third Heaven

As mentioned earlier, the third heaven is Paradise, which is the realm of the spirit. Simply put, this is God's address! It is the world of absolute perfection, absolute peace, absolute authority, and absolute obedience to the will of God. There is no rebellion or spiritual warfare in the realm of the spirit. It is also the place where all things are possible. The realm of the spirit is a perfect reflection of the mind of God, and as a result, it can be classified as **ultimate reality**.

Further biblical evidence of three realities

To reiterate, the universe is composed of three realms, dimensions or realities:

The First Heaven

- The physical realm
- Physical reality

The Second Heaven
- The realm of the mind
- Collective conscious and
- Personal Reality

The Third Heaven
- The realm of the spirit
- Ultimate reality

Further biblical evidence of these three realms can be gleaned from the Genesis account of the 'Tower of Babel.' Set at a time when everyone on earth spoke the same language, this account is unassumingly rich in the dynamics of differing dimensions of reality. As a result, we see God preventing the tower from being built although it had already been built!

Now the whole earth had one language and one speech. And it came to pass, as they journeyed from the east, that they found a plain in the land of Shinar, and they dwelt there. Then they said to one another, "Come, let us make bricks and bake them thoroughly." They had brick for stone, and they had asphalt for mortar. And they said, "Come, let us build ourselves a city, and a tower whose top is in the heavens; let us make a name for ourselves, lest we be scattered abroad over the face of the whole earth." But the Lord came down to see the city and the tower, which the sons of men had built. And the Lord said, "Indeed the people are one and they all have one language, and this is what they begin to do; now nothing that they imagine to do will be withheld from them. Come, let Us go down and there confuse their language, that they may not understand one another's speech." So the Lord scattered

Firstly, **from where did the Lord come down?** He came
down from the place of His abode, **the Third Heaven.**
Secondly, **to where did He come down?** Well, the Bible
says the Lord came down to see a building that was *built.*
When something is built it is *finished.* However, when the
Lord had confused the language of the people, the Bible
states that they "left off from *building* the city." Is this a
contradiction? Certainly not! The Lord did indeed see
a building that was complete, not physically, but in the
collective conscience of the people. The tower was a reality
brought about by their *imagination.* We know this to be so
because in His judgment against the building of the tower,
He made this profound statement, *"Indeed the people are one
and they all have one language, and this is what they begin
to do; now nothing that they imagine to do will be withheld
from them."* The drastic actions God took in preventing the
people from physically building the tower, not only signifies
how real collective conscious is, but also the immeasurable
power of our own thoughts and imagination.

So it was the **Second Heaven** that the Lord came down
to visit. It was in this realm that God saw the completed
tower and made His judgment against it. In pronouncing

His judgment, the Lord said, *"Come, let Us go down and there confuse their language, that they may not understand one another's speech."*

So **where is the Lord going down to?** As He was in the second Heaven, it stands to reason that He intends to go down to the **First Heaven** [the physical realm] to execute His judgment. It is there that God confused the language of the people, and it is there that we see an *unfinished* building abandoned.

Principle Points:

1. The universe is composed of three realms:

   - **The Physical realm**
     The First Heaven

   - **The realm of the mind**
     The Second Heaven

   - **The realm of the spirit**
     The Third Heaven

2. There is no rebellion or spiritual warfare in the realm of the spirit.

3. The realm of the mind is a greater reality than physical reality.

4. The realm of the mind is the 'space' and dimension of our universe from which mental laws operate.

5. Reality is the product of what you believe.

6. We live in a world that is not only subject to our own sense of reality, but also forged and shaped by the thoughts and personal reality of others.

7. The physical realm is where spiritual things are manifested into physical things.

Chapter 2

THE THREE DIMENSIONS OF MAN

For what man knows the thoughts of a man except the spirit of the man which is in him...

$\mathbf{M}$an is a tripartite being. He is composed of the non-corporeal elements of **spirit** and **soul**, nested within a **physical body**. His physical part, the body, is uniquely designed to help him navigate and interact with the physical world, through the senses of touch, smell, sight and sound. Our bodies have it's own nature (the flesh nature) which has an entirely different objective from that of our spirit. The nature of the flesh is *self-preservation* as it is only focused on it's own needs, comfort and gratification. This was no accident! Our bodies were designed that way to ensure that we have the strong survival instincts required to live in the natural realm. For this reason the body represents man's lower nature.

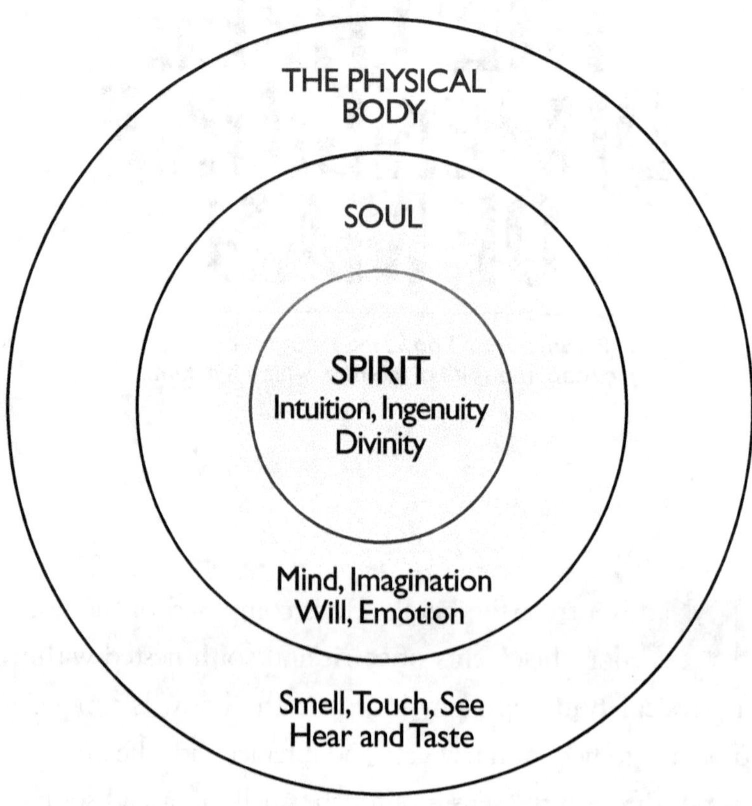

The tripartite make-up of man

In contrast, man's spirit, or what is otherwise called his super conscious mind, is his higher or *divine* self. It is the organ where intuitive knowledge flows and is the source of man's brilliance, ingenuity, genius, and creativity. It is also the part that gives him a sense of divine purpose. The spirit of man is the very essence of his being through which God imparts knowledge, wisdom, and vision. When I speak of vision, I refer to that which is seen in your heart, not your eyes. Vision is tantamount to *spiritual insight*. With vision you will see beyond how things appear and think with foresight well beyond your present time. This fact may not seem so incredulous when we consider the great minds and creative geniuses that were considered to be ahead of their time. Great minds such as Leonardo Da Vinci, the painter, sculptor, architect, musician, scientist, mathematician, engineer, inventor and anatomist. Born in 1452, he was a man of great vision and insight who employed empirical methods that were considered unusual for his time. He conceptualized a helicopter, a tank, concentrated solar power, and amongst other things, a calculator. According to art historian Helen Gardner, the scope and depth of his interests were without precedent and "his mind and personality seem to us superhuman." What appears to be superhuman, however, is in fact the spiritual nature and quality that is innate in us all.

The soul of man is the organ that gives him self-consciousness. It is also the part that reveals his personality. Comprising of mind, free will, and emotion, it serves as the meeting-point and interface for both spirit and body. It is only through the soul that spirit and body can cooperate, as the two by their very nature cannot interact with one another. Therefore, the soul is the most pivotal of all three dimensions of a person. It is the intermediary between the spiritual and physical life. It is only in the soul that the impulses and sensation sensed by the body have any meaning. In addition, the soul and by extension the mind can sense the inner promptings of the super-conscious and receive intuitive knowledge and divine wisdom.

Therefore your soul and by extension 'your heart' is the center-stage of your life. The word heart is a translation from both the Greek and Hebrew word for 'mind.' Not the conscious mind however, but the **subconscious mind**. Your heart is the most 'truthful' part of you. Truthful in the sense that it reveals your true thoughts, beliefs, affections, priorities, state, or condition. Often times the true state of your heart is concealed by the mask of your outer persona. However, the decisions you make, especially under dire or stressful conditions reveals the true state of your heart. It is only what you think in your heart that determines who you are or what you will become. That said - your life is a perfect reflection of the state of your heart.

- Everything you have, came from your heart.
- Everything you lost, was due to your heart.
- Everything you have experienced was because of your heart.
- Everything in your world rests on the state and condition of your heart!

This may not be an easy thing to accept, especially if your life currently reflects much of what you *do not* want. However, what this also means is that your heart gives you an incredible amount of control over your life and the *outcomes* you desire to see. Your heart is the soil for what has and will be *manifested* in your life. It is the arena where your future will be forged. By your own free will you can choose to follow the higher nature of your spirit or choose to live by the lower nature of the flesh. However, the determining factor however, will depend largely on your sense of vision. We are either guided by vision or misguided by a lack of it.

Living in 3 Worlds

Given the divine make-up of man, we can see that he was designed to live simultaneously in 3 worlds. With his body he can interact with the physical world. With his mind, he interacts with the realm of mind and imagination.

Ultimately, he is supposed to interact with God with his spirit. In this way, man has the ability to receive things from heavenly places and manifest them on the earth. This ability is unique only to mankind. No other creature on earth or in heaven has been endowed with this ability.

Principle Points:

1. Man is a tripartite being composed of spirit, soul, and a physical body.

2. The spirit of man is his higher or divine self. It is the source of his brilliance, ingenuity, genius, and creativity.

3. The spirit of man is the very essence of his being through which God imparts knowledge, wisdom, and vision.

4. Your soul is the intermediary between spiritual and physical life.

5. It is only what you think in your heart that determines who you are or what you will become.

6. You were designed to live simultaneously in 3 worlds – the realm of the spirit, the realm of the mind and the physical realm.

7. Due to your design you have the ability to receive things from heavenly places and manifest them on the earth. No other creature on earth or in heaven has been endowed with this ability.

Chapter 3

THE ORIGIN OF THINGS

*Things which are seen were not made
of things which are visible...*

On the subject of the origin of things, the Bible makes it clear that, "The worlds were framed by the **word of God,** so that the things which are seen were not made of things which are visible." (Hebrews 11:3)

The word of God is the spiritual DNA, building block and fabric of the universe. It is the means by which all things were made. Even science agrees that all things on a subatomic level are constructed and held together by an *unseen* and *intangible* force or energy. Careful study of Hebrews 11:3 in its original Greek language reveals that every moment, every situation, and every circumstance, was created, put in place and framed by the word of God. However what are words? Words are in essence *images* in the form of thoughts. If you don't believe me just string a sentence together and tell me what comes to mind! Words are but spiritual containers for images. When you receive a parcel in the post, you know that you have to remove the outer wrapping in order to receive what the sender wants you to have. Likewise, it is the image that you need to receive when the word is delivered. If words are in essence images in the form of thoughts, the word of God is, therefore, images in the form of divine thoughts. That is why the Bible is so rich in metaphors, imagery, symbols, and allegories, all showing the mind of God in pictures and images.

Image is everything!

Therefore, image is the underlying *substance* by which all things are made. Veiled in the invisible form of thought, it is the very substance of our hopes and dreams. The person that coined the phrase 'image is everything' was profoundly correct, as every moment, situation and circumstance were framed by images in the invisible form divine thought. As a result, things that can be seen were made of things [images] that cannot be seen (with the naked eye). What is of great significance is the fact that images carried by words can only be seen once captured on the screen of imagination. When this happens the image now becomes a vision.

So, the word of God, by which all things were made, equates to images in the form of thoughts. These thoughts or images are unseen until captured on the screen of our imagination. Once captured, unseen images now become a visible vision. Vision, therefore, is the *pure language* of God. That is why God often communicates and reveal things to man through dreams and visions. This also explains why much of the prophetic writings and forewarnings made by the Old Testament Prophets emanated from visions. One such example can be seen when an angel appeared to Zachariah:

Now the angel who talked with me came back and wakened me, as a man who is wakened out of his sleep. And he said to me, "What do you see?" So I said, "I am looking, and there is a lampstand of solid gold with a bowl on top of it, and on the stand seven lamps with seven pipes to the seven lamps. Two olive trees are by it, one at the right of the bowl and the other at its left." So I answered and spoke to the angel who talked with me, saying, "What are these, my lord?" Then the angel who talked with me answered and said to me, "Do you not know what these are?" And I said, "No, my lord." So he answered and said to me: "This is the word of the Lord to Zerubbabel: 'Not by might nor by power, but by My Spirit,' Says the Lord of hosts. (Zachariah 4:1-6)

When the angel asked Zachariah "what do you see?" he described a mystically allegoric vision consisting of a lampstand, a bowl, seven lamps, seven pipes, and two olive trees. The angel then asked Zachariah if he knew what these things are. When Zachariah said "no my Lord" the angel said, **"this is the word of the Lord** to Zerubbabel…"

So we see here a direct definition given to a vision, that being the word of God. A vision from God is therefore 'a word' from God. It is important to note that prophets are not the only people that receive visions from God. There are many accounts in the Bible where God speaks through visions and dreams to people from all walks of life. Whether they were Kings or shepherds, soldiers or astrologers, butlers or bakers. None of us are exempt from receiving visions or dreams from God. Indeed God declares in the scriptures,

"I will pour out My Spirit on all flesh; Your sons and your daughters shall prophesy, Your old men shall dream dreams, Your young men shall see visions." (Joel 2:28)

The nature of Light

Another way of understanding why vision is the language of God is through the simple nature of light. The primary nature of light is to cause you to see, or to reveal what is hidden in darkness. Simply put, to give you vision.

Figuratively speaking, when you can see what you could not see before, then you know that light has *spoken* to you. God is light! His nature, therefore, is to cause you to see. God desires to reveal mysteries, secrets, future events, and many hidden truths to those who desire to see what He sees.

Redefining the Word

As we have primarily defined the word of God as vision, in order to grasp where things originate from let us read Hebrews 11:3 again, substituting the text 'word of God' with the word 'vision.'

"By faith we understand that the worlds were framed by vision, so that the things which are seen were not made of things which are visible." (Hebrews 11:3).

Now the true significance and power of vision is revealed:

- Visions have creative and life giving power and are the means by which all things were made.
- Nothing exists that did not first exist as a vision.

Therefore, we live in a universe that was created, shaped and framed by vision.

Principle Points:

1. The word of God is the spiritual DNA, building block and fabric of the universe.

2. Words are in essence images in the form of thoughts.

3. Image is the underlying substance by which all things are made. As a result, things that can be seen were made of images that cannot be seen with the naked eye.

4. The word of God equates to images in the form of thoughts. These images are unseen until captured on the screen of our imagination. Once captured, it becomes a vision.

5. Vision is the pure language of God. When you can see what you could not see before, then you know God has spoken to you.

6. Visions have life giving power and are the means by which all things were made.

7. Nothing exists that did not first exist as a vision.

Chapter 4

THE SIGNIFICANCE OF VISION

*Look now toward heaven, and count the stars
if you are able to number them...*

A vision, in most cases, is a heavenly reality that God wants manifested in the earth. The component central to making this happen is the imagination of man's heart. As explained the imagination of the heart are your inner eyes. It is also where the dominant vision for your life exists. The significance of our imagination is such that God's redemptive plan for mankind stood on one man's ability to see with it.

Abraham's Vision of the Promise

When Abram first encountered God (his name was later changed to Abraham), he was given a life changing command and promise. God told him to

"Get out of your country, from your family and from your father's house, to a land that I will show you. I will make you a great nation; I will bless you and make your name great; and you shall be a blessing. I will bless those who bless you, and I will curse him who curses you; and in you all the families of the earth shall be blessed" (Genesis 12:1-3).

The promise given to Abraham had multiple components, including the promise of many descendants, eminence, divine protection and that Abraham through his descendants would be a blessing to all people. The promise given to Abraham was both physical and spiritual in nature. Physically, Abraham's descendants would become a great nation. The spiritual blessing to *all people* was fulfillled in the coming of Jesus, the Messiah, a descendant of Abraham, through whom people of all nationalities may receive salvation. This was a promise that required great faith from Abraham seeing that he had no children and his wife was barren.

After these things the word of the Lord came to Abram in a vision, saying, "Do not be afraid, Abram. I am your shield, your exceedingly great reward." But Abram said, "Lord God, what will You give me, seeing I go childless, and the heir of my house is Eliezer of Damascus?" Then Abram said, "Look,

You have given me no offspring; indeed one born in my house is my heir!" And behold, the word of the Lord came to him, saying, "This one shall not be your heir, but one who will come from your own body shall be your heir." Then He brought him outside and said, "Look now toward heaven, and count the stars if you are able to number them." And He said to him, "So shall your descendants be." And he believed in the Lord, and He accounted it to him for righteousness. (Genesis 15:1-6)

In order to reaffirm the promise, the Lord visited Abraham again to quell his fears. When Abraham expressed his concerns that the child of his servant Eliezer would become his heir, the Lord brought Abraham outside so that he could look towards heaven and count the stars. The numeracy of the stars acted as a metaphoric vision enabling Abraham to imagine the enormity of his offspring. From that moment on, Abraham's thoughts and imagination were fueled by what he saw in the night sky. The vision he now had transformed him into a 'Father of Nations' despite the fact that he and his wife were childless and advanced in years.

Not only did Abraham become the Father of Nations but also the Father of Faith. When he captured 'the vision of the promise' the night stars presented in his imagination, he then **believed** that what he saw would become a physical reality. That is the very act of faith. Many people define faith as a belief in something you cannot see. However, the truth is the direct opposite. Faith is the actions you take according to what you see in the imagination of your heart. That is why God credited Abraham's belief in the vision presented to mind as *righteousness*. Righteousness is a product of faith. It is the attribute and status conferred or imputed on someone who believes in what God has promised. Promises that God gives to men and women through vision.

Therefore, Abraham became righteous due to his belief in his vision! What is most profound is the fact that this whole encounter took place in a vision:

After these things the word of the Lord came to Abram in a vision... (Genesis 15:1)

Therefore the acts of Abraham:

- complaining to God,
- coming outside of his tent,
- looking towards heaven,
- seeing the vision of the promise presented by the stars
- believing that the vision would become a reality

all took place *within* a vision. Abraham, therefore, became righteous by believing in a vision within a vision! More importantly, Abraham's belief enabled the vision to become the *seed* and *blueprint* for the manifestation of God's redemptive plan. In the same way a house is not built without a blueprint, a reality cannot be manifest with the blueprint of vision.

Abraham's Vision of the Ultimate Sacrifice

Another critical moment pertinent to the redemptive plan for mankind was when God told Abraham to sacrifice his only son Isaac.

Now it came to pass after these things that God tested Abraham, and said to him, "Abraham!" And he said, "Here I am." Then He said, "Take now your son, your only son Isaac, whom you love, and go to the land of Moriah, and offer him there as a burnt offering on one of the mountains of which I shall tell you." So Abraham rose early in the morning and saddled his donkey, and took two of his young men with him, and Isaac his son; and he split the wood for the burnt offering, and arose and went to the place of which God had told him. Then on the third day Abraham lifted his eyes and saw the place afar off. And Abraham said to his young men, "Stay here with the donkey; the lad and I will go yonder and worship, and we will come back to you." So Abraham took the wood of the burnt offering and laid it on Isaac his son; and he took the fire in his hand, and a knife, and the two of them went together. But Isaac spoke to Abraham his father and said, "My father!" And he said, "Here I am, my son." Then he said, "Look, the fire and the wood, but where is the lamb for a burnt offering?" And Abraham said, "My son, God will provide for Himself the lamb for a burnt offering." So the two of them went together. Then they came to the place of which God had told him. And Abraham built an altar there and placed the wood in order; and he bound Isaac his son and laid him on the altar, upon the wood. And Abraham stretched

out his hand and took the knife to slay his son. But the Angel of the Lord called to him from heaven and said, "Abraham, Abraham!" So he said, "Here I am." And He said, "Do not lay your hand on the lad, or do anything to him; for now I know that you fear God, since you have not withheld your son, your only son, from Me." Then Abraham lifted his eyes and looked, and there behind him was a ram caught in a thicket by its horns. So Abraham went and took the ram, and offered it up for a burnt offering instead of his son. (Genesis 22:1-13)

God told Abraham to sacrifice his *only* son [Isaac], even though He had said, "it is through Isaac that your offspring will be reckoned" (Genesis 21:12). In light of the promise God had made, can you imagine what was going through Abraham's mind? It would be understandable if he had a lot of confusion, doubts or even anger. However, this was not the case. Firstly, when Abraham arrived near the mountain, note what he said to the young men that accompanied him, "Stay here with the donkey; the lad and I will go yonder and worship, and **we will come back to you**." Although Abraham intended to sacrifice his son in obedience to God, he expected Isaac to come back with him! How could he have such an expectation? Although not shown in Genesis, the book of Hebrews answers this question, shedding light on what was actually going on in Abraham's mind.

By faith Abraham, when God tested him, offered Isaac as a sacrifice. He who had embraced the promises was about to sacrifice his one and only son, even though God had said to him, "It is through Isaac that your offspring will be reckoned."

Abraham reasoned that God could even raise the dead, and so in a manner of speaking he did receive Isaac back from death. (Hebrews 11:17-19 NIV)

What was so amazing about Abraham's faith is the conclusion he came to because of God's promise to him. He reasoned that if God required Him to sacrifice his son, then the only course of action left would be for God to raise Isaac from the dead! **This is what Abraham imagined God doing.** Sometimes God puts you in situations to challenge the promises He made to you. He does this in order for you to give birth to a vision. That vision when conceived in the imagination becomes the template or blueprint for the promise He wants manifested in your physical life or in the lives of others.

I believe that God commanded Abraham to sacrifice his son, not only to test his faith, but also to generate the vision of a son [Isaac] being sacrificed by the hand of his own father [Abraham], only to be ressurected from the dead by God! This was a vision that could only be crafted by Abraham's faith. This vision was a mental reality. In other words, as far as God was concerned, this is what actually happened. God brought about this vision because the covenant He had with Abraham *demanded* that what happens to Abraham's son must also happen to God's son. God, therefore, used the vision created in Abraham's imagination as the blueprint for mankind's redemption through the death and resurrection of His only son, Jesus.

Abraham's experience with God underscores the true role and significance of imagination. What we see through the eyes of our heart is more real than what we see with our eyes. That is why God uses our imagination to manifest His plans. When a vision is embraced, it becomes the blueprint for shaping and creating the future. Every great act that has positively impacted human history was a result of the combined role of vision and imagination.

Principle Points:

1. A vision is a heavenly reality that God wants manifested on the earth.

2. When Abraham captured the vision of the promise in his imagination, he believed that what he saw would become a physical reality.

3. What we see through the eyes of our heart is more real than what we see with our eyes.

4. Sometimes God puts you in situations to challenge the promises He made to you. He does this in order for you to give birth to a vision.

5. When a vision is embraced it becomes the blueprint for shaping and creating the future.

6. God used the vision of Abraham's imagination as the blueprint for mankind's redemption.

7. Every great act that has positively impacted human history was a result of the vision captured by imagination.

VISION

Chapter 5

MANKIND DEFINED

*Nothing will be restrained from them,
which they have imagined to do....*

**"The kingdom of heaven is like treasure hidden in a field.
When a man found it, he hid it again, and then in his joy went
and sold all he had and bought that field." (Matthew 13:44)**

For many years, I have pondered over this curious parable shared by Jesus. Why did the "treasure seeker" hide the treasure he found, back in the same place he found it? Could he not have taken the treasure away for himself? Why would he go to the extreme of selling *all* that he had to buy *the field*?

Was it not the owner of the field who hid the treasure in the first place? If so, surely he would know that in selling the field he would lose his treasure? Maybe the answer lies in the owner not knowing the true value of what was hidden in his field? Moreover, perhaps what was treasure to the buyer was of no value to the owner? That being the case, this treasure could not have been gold, rubies or anything else we would instantly recognize as treasure. Instead, this treasure must be something of great value to one who recognizes its true *potential*. Then it hit me: in the same way, your potential cannot be separated from your person, maybe the treasure could not be separated from the field. This treasure was not merely hidden in the field - **it was embedded**. Therefore, the value of the treasure was inextricably linked to the field. That is why the treasure seeker could not take away the treasure but instead bought the field.

If this treasure was not gold, rubies, or any other precious stone, what was it, and why was it so valuable to the treasure seeker? If we look at the word 'treasure' in the original Greek language it was written in, we find the word 'thesauros.' This is where the English word 'thesaurus' is derived from. Thesauros refers to a casket, receptacle or storehouse in which valuables are kept. It is not the treasure itself but only the place where the treasure is kept. Why would a container be considered treasure, especially if it were empty? The answer lies in the *function* of the container. For example, if you were in a desert, the most valuable thing you would need is water. Water, in this case, is a treasure. But you would also need a *suitable container* for the water so that you could quench your thirst as you journeyed across the desert. As a result, the container would have the same value to you as the water itself. Likewise, the 'storehouse' hidden in the field was indeed treasure because of what it was able to contain.

So what was this storehouse, and what made it so valuable? To find this out we must first understand what the field symbolized. If we look at other parables Jesus shared and interpreted, we find that any reference to the ground or field referred to people, or more precisely 'the heart.' As mentioned earlier, your heart represents your subconscious or inner mind, the part of you that reflects your true thoughts and beliefs. It is the place, which forms and manifests your personal reality. If the field represents your heart, what is embedded in your heart that is of such great value? The answer is **your imagination**.

Imagination of the heart

As explained earlier, imagination is the only organ capable of seeing images hidden in the invisible form of thought.

When God shows us a vision it is shown on the screen of our imagination. However, the imagination I speak of is the imagination of the heart. The imagination of the heart is your 'inner eye.' It is the imagination of your subconscious mind and should not be confused with the casual and fleeting imaginings of your conscious mind. In the world-renowned classic book 'Think And Grow Rich,' Napoleon Hill defines two forms of imagination: synthetic and creative imagination. Synthetic imagination merely works with the material of experience, education, and observation with which it is fed. Creative imagination, however, is the faculty through which "hunches" and "inspirations" are received. Through the faculty of creative imagination, the finite mind of man has direct communication with Infinite Intelligence. It is by this faculty that all basic, or new ideas are handed over to man. The imagination of our hearts is the source of our creativity. It is the seedbed for the future you are destined to create. What you see with the inner eyes of your heart is vitally more important than what you see with your physical eyes. To quote J. Oswald Sanders:

"Eyes that look are common. Eyes that see are rare."

Man's imagination is the only suitable container for transporting 'spiritual things' from heaven so that they may become physical things on earth. These 'things' are important solutions vital for mankind's progress, deliverance, prosperity, and peace. Things such as witty inventions, innovative services, knowledge that leads to medical breakthroughs, technological breakthroughs, a new way of thinking, and so much more. In a nutshell, spiritual things reflect wisdom from above. According to the scriptures, wisdom is infinitely more precious than silver and gold.

"Wisdom is the principal thing; therefore get wisdom: and with all thy getting get understanding." (Proverbs 4:7)

"How much better is it to get wisdom than gold! and to get understanding rather to be chosen than silver!" (Proverbs 16:16)

"Buy the truth, and sell it not; also wisdom, and instruction, and understanding." (Proverbs 23:23)

Therefore, Divine Wisdom is a heavenly treasure. It is expressed by means of vision [the word of God] and is brought to earth through the imagination of the heart. As a result, your imagination is your most precious possession. It is the treasure that is buried in your heart and the means by which your dreams can become real.

Seeing the impossible

Imagination is the means by which mankind achieves. In other words, we achieve what we see. We can achieve infinitely more from what we see in our hearts than what others tell us to do. The power of imagination is such that nothing can restrain you from doing what you imagine to do. This is because imagination is the only part of us that does not recognize impossibilities. If I told you to imagine yourself flying like superman, you would do so. If I said it was impossible for you to walk on water, you would imagine yourself doing just that! If I said there's no such thing as a green elephant with pink spots, in an instant a green elephant with pink spots would appear in your mind. Your imagination was created this way for the higher purpose of realizing your God-given vision.

As mentioned, a vision is a blueprint for making the impossible possible. This starts with the belief that this will happen. As with Abraham, your belief must be based on the ability to visualize a reality that would generally be perceived as impossible. The only faculty able to do this is your imagination.

The Visionary

In answering the question of what is man, we can derive an answer from the following points:

- Man consists of elements of three worlds -
  Spirit, Mind, and Matter

- Man was designed to live and interact
  in three worlds - Spirit, Mind, and Matter

- Man has the ability to materialize a heavenly reality
  by visualizing it in his imagination and
  manifesting it on earth through a set path
  - Spirit, to Mind, to Matter.

Man is a divine creature, formed in the image of God, created to manifest things from Heaven to Earth. He is able to do this because he was created to be a bridge between three worlds. No other creature is equipped to create and shape the future by bringing a slice of heaven to earth or manifesting a God-given vision. That being the case, man was uniquely created to be a visionary. By definition, a visionary is someone who thinks about or plans the future with imagination and wisdom. Not only are we to plan the future but also to create the future. The value of your imagination is more than you can perceive. With it, God desires to manifest His vision for mankind. That is why, like the treasure seeker, He gave His all to redeem not just your heart but also your imagination. Your imagination is key to the future you were destined to manifest. Not just for yourself, but for your family, your nation and your world.

It is important to note that a person who has a vision but does not do anything to materialize what he or she sees is just a dreamer, not a visionary. You were created to be a visionary. Therefore, if you are not actively materializing vision(s) placed on your heart, you are missing the very purpose of your existence.

Principle Points:

1. The imagination of the heart is your 'inner eye.'

2. The imagination of the heart is the faculty through which "hunches" and "inspirations" are received.

3. Through the imagination of the heart, the finite mind of man has direct communication with Infinite Intelligence.

4. The power of imagination is such that nothing can restrain you from doing what you imagine to do.

5. Man is a divine creature, formed in the image of God, created to manifest things from Heaven to Earth.

6. Your imagination is key to the future you were destined to manifest.

7. Man was uniquely created to be a visionary.

PART TWO

MANIFESTING YOUR VISION

INTRO

We are creatures that function by *image and imagination*. Our whole world is swayed by how we handle, process, and manifest images. What you see through the eyes of your imagination is the key to releasing your *creative power*. It is through your imagination that God imparts vision. A vision is a heavenly reality that God wants manifested on earth. Once this heavenly reality has gripped your imagination, it becomes your passion, purpose, and destiny. When I say heavenly reality, I am simply referring to *what God says is possible*. With God, all things are possible! That is the mantra and reality of heaven. Vision, therefore, is the *blueprint* for making the impossible possible. It is because of vision that mankind has always been able to achieve what at the time was considered impossible. Without vision, we would all be trapped a world of self-limitation. Therefore, as a visionary, it is imperative that you discover the key to fulfillling your destiny and understand the process by which vision is manifested.

Chapter 6

FAITH IN YOUR VISION

*Faith is the substance of things hoped for,
the evidence of things not seen...*

Faith and belief are often used interchangeably because you cannot have faith without belief. However, the fact that you don't need faith to believe that something is true shows that there is a distinct difference. For example, you don't need faith to believe that the world is round. Even before man could rocket into space and see the earth as a whole, there was enough evidence to substantiate that fact. However, believing that God created the world does require faith. This is because the belief in 'creation' is largely based on **evidence** that cannot be physically seen.

So faith differs from belief based on the ability to see. If your belief is based on what can be physically seen, then your belief is void of faith. However, if your belief is based on what cannot be seen, or physically identified, then your belief is based on faith. That being the case, the term 'blind faith' is a misnomer! Faith enables us to see what cannot be seen through the physical senses. It is inextricably linked to your vision. The clearer you are about what you can mentally see, the stronger your faith. Any information (words) that enables you to have a clearer vision or image of what you want to achieve strengthens your faith.

Having given Abraham a promise, God strengthened Abraham's faith in the promise by giving him a specific vision:

"Look now toward heaven, and count the stars if you are able to number them." And He said to him, "So shall your descendants be." (Genesis 15:5)

From that day on, Abraham's thoughts were fueled by what he saw in the night sky. The stars he saw made the innumerable amount of descendants he would have a mental reality; despite the fact that he and his wife were childless and advanced in years.

It was the vision that inspired *hope* in Abraham, which in turn strengthened his faith. The Bible succinctly tells us that, *"faith is the substance of things hoped for, the evidence of things not seen" (Hebrews 11:1)*. If faith is the substance of things hoped for, and vision inspires hope, then it stands to reason that faith and vision are one and the same! Vision is the essence of faith. There is no faith without a corresponding vision. If this concept of faith appears too radical, it is because we often define faith by its works or attributes such as a complete trust, confident expectation or a strong belief in God. Although these attributes are integral to exercising faith, they do not represent the essence of faith. Trust, confidence, expectation, and a strong belief in something yet to be manifested all spawn from the vision you see on the inside. The vision within is what gives life to great acts of faith. It was the vision inside Martin Luther King Jr. (as expressed in his famed 'I had a dream' speech) that galvanized millions of Americans and broke the back of racial inequality.

The fact that faith and by extension vision is the 'substance' of things hoped for, supports my earlier assertion that 'image' is the underlying substance by which all things are made. There is nothing that has been made that did not first begin as an image. Every outcome has its genesis in an intangible image. Veiled in the invisible form of thought, it is the very substance of our hopes, dreams and reality.

Faith vs Fantasy

Although faith is in essence the image of a desired outcome, it is vital to distinguish whose desire I am referring to. The Bible informs us that faith comes by hearing, and hearing the word of God (Romans 10:17). In other words faith is a projection of God's desire. It is the future and the outcome He wants you to see, receive and manifest in your life and this physical world. **Anything other than that resides in the realm of fantasy.** Faith requires you to align your desires with God's desires, and position yourself (spiritually) to see what God wants you to see. Fantasy however, is simply about manifesting your ego and selfish desires. Further more, fantasies are desires that emanate from 'circumstance' rather than what God has placed in your heart. Often times we allow our circumstances to dictate who we are instead of expressing who we are to change our circumstances. This can only be done through the manifestation of faith.

Principle Points:

1. Vision is the essence of faith. There is no faith without a corresponding vision.

2. Faith enables us to see what cannot be seen through the physical senses. The clearer you are about what you can mentally see, the stronger your faith.

3. The vision within is what gives life to great acts of faith.

4. Image is the substance of things hoped for.

5. Every outcome has its genesis in an intangible image.

6. Faith requires you to align your desires with God's desires, and see what God wants you to see.

Chapter 7

DON'T LOOK UP, LOOK WITHIN!

Set your mind on things above, not on things on the earth...

God designed and assigned men and women to be visionaries. By design we are made from the essential elements of three worlds: physicality, imagination [mind], and spirit. This enables us to interact between all three realms, and take things from spiritual dimensions and manifest them into physical reality. It is commonplace for individuals to pursue the dreams and imaginations of their own minds. However, each of us has a higher purpose in bringing a heavenly reality to Earth. In order for you to do that, you must first realize that contrary to common perception, Heaven [the realm of the spirit] does not exist above the clouds, beyond space, or on anywhere on the apex of the physical world. In other words, Heaven is not above! Heaven is an inner reality and experience.

The story of the Tower of Babel gives an account of what happened when God came down to see the city and the tower that the people had built [explained in chapter 2]. With the safe assumption that His starting position was the third Heaven, the fact that He descended into the conscious realm of man's thoughts and imagination indicates that Heaven is a higher state of consciousness and reality. This could be the reason why God derailed the building of a tower being built for the sole purpose of touching heaven. Allowing such a tower to be built would have endorsed a search for divinity in the wrong direction.

When the Bible refers to God being 'on high,' it has nothing to do with Him dwelling externally above us. Instead, it refers to Him existing on the highest plain of consciousness, awareness, perception and understanding. Therefore we 'look up' to God with our minds and not with our eyes. As Paul says *"seek those things which are above, where Christ is, sitting at the right hand of God. Set your mind on things above, not on things on the earth"* (Colossians 3:1-2). Further biblical evidence supporting the fact that Heaven is an inner reality can be found in Paul's account of being caught up to the third heaven.

It is doubtless not profitable for me to boast. I will come to visions and revelations of the Lord: I know a man in Christ who fourteen years ago -whether in the body I do not know, or whether out of the body I do not know, God knows - such a one was caught up to the third heaven. And I know such a man - whether in the body or out of the body I do not know, God knows how he was caught up into Paradise and heard inexpressible words, which it is not lawful for a man to utter. (2 Corinthians 12:1-4)

As identified in the text, Paul's experience of being caught up to the third heaven was described in the context of **visions and revelations** from the Lord. In other words, he experienced heaven through a vision! The reality of the vision was such that Paul did not know if he was out of his body or not. This goes to show that Heaven is a realm that can be reached from within. It also stands to reason that Heaven is a reality that can be experienced in the **here-and-now**, not just in the hereafter.

Look Within

True visionaries are those who look within instead of without. They can see heavenly realities [vision] revealed in their hearts and manifest them in the earth. They trust the vision and allow it to guide their thoughts, decision, and direction. They live by an **internal locus of control** rather than external. In the field of personal psychology, the principle of 'locus of control' was developed by Julian Rotter in 1954 and refers to the extent to which individuals believe they can control events affecting them. Studies have shown that people with a high external locus of control believe that control over events and what other people do is outside them, and that they personally have little or no control over such things. On the other hand, individuals with a strong internal locus of control believe in their own ability to control themselves and influence events around them.

Many people operate from an external locus of control by looking (outward) to the stars, moon planets, or even the universe to direct their path, fulfilll their desires and determine their future. They exercise the law of attraction by *speaking* to the universe, telling the universe what they want and believing they will receive it. The universe, in this case, is portrayed as a cosmic genie, ready to grant us the desires of our hearts. Although the law of attraction does work, I take a different view on where true power lies.

Firstly, from a biblical standpoint, the spiritual power or system of the universe is the Kingdom of Heaven. Jesus' entire teaching and focus was dedicated to expressing the Kingdom. He told parables to help understand and discover the Kingdom. He performed miracles in order to demonstrate the Kingdom. His death, burial, and resurrection, was for the purpose of giving mankind the Kingdom. However, out of all that Jesus revealed about the Kingdom, the most profound was His declaration that the Kingdom of God operates from within.

Now when He was asked by the Pharisees when the kingdom of God would come, He answered them and said, "The kingdom of God does not come with observation; nor will they say, 'See here!' or 'See there!' For indeed, the kingdom of God is within you." (Luke 17:20-21 NKJV)

The true nature of the Kingdom is power, emanating from the hearts of men and women. It is the Kingdom within that responds to our deepest and strongest desires. That is why we are able to attract whatever is in alignment with our dominant thoughts.

Secondly, as mentioned, you consist of all the three realms of the universe, that being spirit, mind, and matter. Therefore, in principle, you are a 'universe' in your own right. The universe we should, therefore, *speak to* is that of ourselves, rather than the perceived *genie* in the cosmos.

These two factors combined show that there is more to being a visionary than we can ever conceive. What is clear is the fact that a true visionary operates from an internal of control. The controlling factor is the vision within his or her heart. It is vision that synergizes the 'Kingdom within' to our divine make up. Everything we need to manifest or vision and achieve our purpose lies within our hearts.

IMPORTANT NOTE

Hopefully you can now see how man is able to stand on earth and reach into Heaven. However it should be noted that man's ability to touch the third Heaven is only possible in Christ. That was the purpose for His death on the cross. It is only through Him and in Him that we gain access. Without Christ we are only limited to the vast reality of mind, thought and imagination.

Principle Points:

1. Heaven is an inner reality and experience.

2. Heaven does not exist above the clouds, beyond space, or on anywhere on the apex of the physical world.

3. When the Bible refers to God being *on high*, it refers to Him existing on the highest plain of consciousness, awareness, perception and understanding.

4. Visionaries operate from an internal locus of control rather than external.

5. Individuals with a strong internal locus of control believe in their own ability to control themselves and influence events around them.

6. The spiritual power or system of the universe is the Kingdom of Heaven. The true nature of this Kingdom is that it operates from the hearts of men and women.

7. As a person that consists of the all the three realms of the universe, in principle, you are a 'universe' in your own right.

Chapter 8

RECOGNIZE WHAT YOU HAVE

Whoever has will be given more, and they will have an abundance. Whoever does not have, even what they have will be taken from them...

A key skill a visionary must have in order to fulfilll their vision is the ability to recognize what they already have. Everything that you experience in life is a result of what you recognized or did not recognize. How you see yourself and the world around you is pivotal to what you will achieve in life. This is because sight is a faculty of the mind, not the eyes. It is your mind that gives meaning to the streams of light and colors that pass through your eyes.

Your eyes serve only as a window that gives *one dimension* of sight to your mind. The meaning you give to anything you encounter will give rise to how you feel about it. How you feel will determine how you will respond or react, which culminates in what you experience. The beauty is that you can 'frame' an event or encounter with a meaning that best suits or empowers you. You can determine whether the event is ultimately positive or negative despite how it initially appears. How you frame the event, will determine what you feel, experience and ultimately achieve.

"People only give up on their dreams when they feel they do not have the opportunity to fulfilll them. However, it is not the absence of opportunities that is the problem, but instead the failure to recognize opportunities and resources that already exist in their lives."

Each and everyone of us are surrounded by a sea of opportunity and the only reason we have not seized it is because we do not see it, and we do not see it because we do not recognize it or we do not see it's value. There are many examples in the Bible of people failing to see what they have:

Elisha and The Pot of Oil

The wife of a man from the company of the prophets cried out to Elisha, "Your servant my husband is dead, and you know that he revered the LORD. But now his creditor is coming to take my two boys as his slaves." Elisha replied to her, "How can I help you? Tell me, what do you have in your house?" **"Your servant has nothing there at all," she said, "except a small jar of olive oil."** Elisha said, "Go around and ask all your neighbors for empty jars. Don't ask for just a few. Then go inside and shut the door behind you and your sons. Pour oil into all the jars, and as each is filled, put it to one side." She left him and shut the door behind her and her sons. They brought the jars to her and she kept pouring. When all the jars were full, she said to her son, "Bring me another one." But he replied, "There is not a jar left." Then the oil stopped flowing. She went and told the man of God, and he said, "Go, sell the oil and pay your debts. You and your sons can live on what is left." (2 Kings 4:1-7)

Elijah and Widow of Zarephath

Then the word of the LORD came to him: "Go at once to Zarephath in the region of Sidon and stay there. I have directed a widow there to supply you with food." So he went to Zarephath. When he came to the town gate, a widow was there gathering sticks. He called to her and asked, "Would you bring me a little water in a jar so I may have a drink?" As she was going to get it, he called, "And bring me, please, a piece of bread." "As surely as the LORD your God lives," she replied, "**I don't have any bread—only a handful of flour in a jar and a little olive oil in a jug.** I am gathering a few sticks to take home and make a meal for myself and my son, that we may eat it—and die." Elijah said to her, "Don't be afraid. Go home and do as you have said. But first make a small loaf of bread for me from what you have and bring it to me, and then make something for yourself and your son. For this is what the LORD, the God of Israel, says: 'The jar of flour will not be used up and the jug of oil will not run dry until the day the LORD sends rain on the land.' " She went away and did as Elijah had told her. So there was food every day for Elijah and for the woman and her family. For the jar of flour was not used up and the jug of oil did not run dry, in keeping with the word

of the LORD spoken by Elijah. (1Kings 17:8-16)

Jesus feeding the 5000 men

When Jesus looked up and saw a great crowd coming toward him, he said to Philip, "Where shall we buy bread for these people to eat?" He asked this only to test him, for he already had in mind what he was going to do. Philip answered him, "It would take more than half a year's wages to buy enough bread for each one to have a bite!" Another of his disciples, Andrew, Simon Peter's brother, spoke up, **"Here is a boy with five small barley loaves and two small fish, but how far will they go among so many?"** Jesus said, "Have the people sit down." There was plenty of grass in that place, and they sat down (about five thousand men were there). Jesus then took the loaves, gave thanks, and distributed to those who were seated as much as they wanted. He did the same with the fish. When they had all had enough to eat, he said to his disciples, "Gather the pieces that are left over. Let nothing be wasted." So they gathered them and filled twelve baskets with the pieces of the five barley loaves left over by those who had eaten. (John 6:5-13)

The emboldened text in each of the scriptures above highlights where people fail to see that what they had is was the key to what they needed. However, in each of the examples a 'miracle' was used to convert what they had to what needed. As the vast majority of us are not proficient at miracle working, how can practical and replicable principles be drawn from these examples?

The Two Pillars of Success

There are times when Jesus taught in the synagogues. The Bible does not say what He taught, but what He said led the listeners to make the following connection:

And when the Sabbath had come, He began to teach in the synagogue. And many hearing Him were astonished, saying, "Where did this Man get these things? And what wisdom is this which is given to Him, that such mighty works are performed by His hands! (Mark 6:2)

The mighty works mentioned here are the miracles Jesus performed. So based on what they heard they made the connection between miracles and wisdom. In other words, the miracles that Jesus performed flowed and emanated from Wisdom. Going back to the scriptural examples mentioned earlier, the principles we can draw from them can be summed up in what I call the two pillars of success:

1. Recognize what you have.

2. Have the wisdom to convert what you have to what you need.

The reason why Jesus, Elisha, and Elijah recognized potential opportunities is because they had the wisdom to convert what they have to what they need, want or desire! When you have the wisdom to convert what you have to what you need you will never ignore things that seem insignificant again.

The Cost of Ignoring What You Have

As a visionary, it is therefore vital for you to recognize what you have otherwise you could fall foul of another spiritual principle of success:

Whoever has will be given more, and they will have an abundance. Whoever does not have, even what they have will be taken from them. (Matthew 13:12)

How can something be taken away from you that you don't have? This can only happen when you fail to recognize what you already have. When you fail to recognize the significance or value of things or persons in your life you will eventually pay the price of them exiting your life.

Principle Points:

1. Everything that you experience in life is a result of what you recognized or did not recognize.

2. How you see yourself and the world around you is pivotal to what you will achieve in life.

3. A sea of opportunity surrounds us all. Unfortunately many do not seize it, because we do not recognize it or we do not see its value.

4. People only give up on their dreams when they feel they do not have the opportunity to fulfilll them. However, it is not the absence of opportunities that is the problem, but instead the failure to recognize opportunities and resources that already exist in their lives.

5. Success is the result of recognizing what you have, and having the wisdom to convert what you have to what you need.

6. When you fail to recognize what you already have, you will lose what you have.

Chapter 9

GET WISDOM

Speak to all who are gifted artisans, whom I have filled with the spirit of wisdom...

Success, therefore, emanates from one's ability to see potential. Your vision is in essence your potential. It is something that you can see every day. However, as explained in the previous chapter, 'seeing' is only one pillar of success. The other pillar is wisdom. In general, wisdom is seen as *good judgment*. However, wisdom is much more than that. Wisdom is the only means by which your vision can become a physical reality. Without it, your vision is just wishful thinking. Therefore, as a visionary, it is essential that you get wisdom. But in order to do that, you have to know what wisdom really is.

Biblical Wisdom

Wisdom from a biblical perspective can be better understood when we apply the law of first mention. The law of first mention is a hermeneutical law used in interpreting ancient books such as the Bible. According to this law, the very first mention of any important word gives that word its most complete, and accurate, meaning, to not only serve as a "key" in understanding the word's biblical concept, but to also provide a foundation for its fuller development in later parts of the Bible. So, if we want to find the true meaning and application of wisdom we have to find where it is first mentioned in the Bible. The first mention of wisdom can be found in the book of Exodus.

In the King James it reads…

"And thou shalt speak unto all that are wise hearted, whom I have filled with the spirit of wisdom, that they may make Aaron's garments to consecrate him, that he may minister unto me in the priest's office." (Exodus 28:3)

The people described as 'wise hearted' in the Bible are the

artisans. Artisans are skilled craftsmen, and individuals with particular creative skills such as: painting, embroidery, engraving, and other creative work. The essential skill of an artisan lies in his or her ability to skillfully manifest particular things captured in their imagination. Once an image or vision is set in their minds, they materialize it through the skillful application of knowledge and understanding. It was this ability that made the artisans so essential to Moses. Not just because of their creative ability but also their ability to manifest 'his' vision. You see, as with all visionaries, Moses was tasked with the job of manifesting on earth what exists in heaven. In this case, he was given a vision of the tabernacle (that exists in heaven) and charged with the responsibility of reproducing it on earth.

...there are priests who offer the gifts according to the law; who serve the copy and shadow of the heavenly things, as Moses was divinely instructed when he was about to make the tabernacle. For He said, "See that you make all things according to the pattern shown you on the mountain." (Hebrews 8:4-5)

It was of vital importance that the tabernacle be reproduced on earth exactly as it was in heaven. Everything about the tabernacle had a symbolic meaning. The furnishings, the fabrics, the colours, and even the wooden pegs were of great symbolic value. Failure to manifest the tabernacle with the accuracy that was required would result in the tabernacle's significance being lost. That is why Moses had to share his vision with individuals whom God had given a spirit of wisdom. Why did God give them a spirit of wisdom? So that may accurately capture Moses' heavenly vision and skilfully manifest on earth. Wisdom therefore is the creative power and process required to capture a heavenly vision and skilfully manifesting it on the earth. It is the means by which the unseen becomes seen, and the intangible becomes tangible. This involves the skilful use of knowledge and understanding for creative works. We see this in the building of the tabernacle when the people were *stirred* by wisdom; having been given knowledge and understanding for creative works.

"All the women who were gifted artisans spun yarn with their hands, and brought what they had spun, of blue, purple, and scarlet, and fine linen. And all the women whose heart stirred with wisdom spun yarn of goats' hair." (Exodus 35:25-26)

Then the Lord spoke to Moses, saying: "See, I have called by name Bezalel the son of Uri, the son of Hur, of the tribe of Judah. And I have filled him with the Spirit of God, in wisdom, in understanding, in knowledge, and in all manner of workmanship, to design artistic works, to work in gold, in silver, in bronze, in cutting jewels for setting, in carving wood, and to work in all manner of workmanship. And I, indeed I, have appointed with him Aholiab the son of Ahisamach, of the tribe of Dan; and I have put wisdom in the hearts of all who are gifted artisans, that they may make all that I have commanded you. The tabernacle of meeting, the ark of the Testimony and the

mercy seat that is on it, and all the furniture of the tabernacle, the table and its utensils, the pure gold lampstand with all its utensils, the altar of incense, the altar of burnt offering with all its utensils, and the laver and its base, the garments of ministry, the holy garments for Aaron the priest and the garments of his sons, to minister as priests, and the anointing oil and sweet incense for the holy place. According to all that I have commanded you they shall do." (Exodus 31:1-11)

Wisdom for your vision

To reiterate, wisdom is the creative power and process required to capture a heavenly vision and skilfully manifesting it on the earth. It was given to artisans endowed with the ability to capture and materialize Moses' God-given vision. It does not matter how imaginative or skilled an artist is, without the required wisdom they will not be able to capture your vision. As a visionary you must have wisdom. Having wisdom however is not just about you informing your mind, but also finding 'wise hearted artisans' to help you. A wise hearted artisan in this case is any individual who is able to capture your vision (or any particular aspect of your vision) and effectively help you bring it to fruition. Their ability to do this is evidence that God has given them 'wisdom for your vision.' As the saying goes, *"it takes teamwork to make the dream work."* Anyone with wisdom for your vision should be on your team! No matter how skilled and knowledgeable you are, you cannot fulfill your vision by yourself. You must, therefore, recognize and develop working relationships with individuals who have *wisdom for your vision.*

Principle Points:

1. Wisdom is the creative power required to capture and manifest a heavenly vision on earth.

2. Wisdom is the means by which the unseen becomes seen, and the intangible becomes tangible.

3. Wisdom is the skilful application of knowledge and understanding.

4. Wisdom is the creative power you.

5. Wisdom is the creative power in others who can help you manifest your vision.

6. Only choose those with wisdom for your vision to be on your team!

Chapter 10

DARE TO DREAM BIG

God has made everything beautiful for its own time.
He has planted eternity in the human heart....

Everyone has a vision or a dream! If you don't have a dream, it is only because you are yet to discover your true passion. Your true passion is your obsession. It is the greatest single clue to your true identity. **Don't develop any life long plans until you discover your true passion!**

When you discover 'your passion,' the very thing you want to achieve, daydreaming will become a common pastime! Although it is often associated with laziness, daydreaming is one of the most productive things you can do with your time. To quote Lupita Nyong'o from her Oscar award winning speech, *"your dreams are valid"* – and indeed they are! Daydreaming allows you to step out of your present reality and 'hang-out' in your future. It is key to bringing about the deepest desires of your heart. Therefore, don't be afraid to dream. More importantly, don't be afraid to dream big! No dream is too big for you! This is because within you lay not only your own dreams and purpose but also eternity!

Eternity

"God has made everything beautiful for its own time. He has planted eternity in the human heart, but even so, people cannot see the whole scope of God's work from beginning to end." (Ecclesiastes 3:11 NLT)

Eternity is the complete picture of God's divine plan and will. The fact that God is able to place eternity in your heart shows that, *like God*, your 'who-ness' cannot be measured and is totally unfathomable. Therefore, give yourself permission to take the limits off yourself, and what you can achieve. If your 'big dream' is but a part of God's plan, then nothing can prevail against you. When you seek to fulfilll your God-given vision, everything will work together for your good. You will achieve what others thought could not be achieved. That is why it is better to manifest vision rather than your own fantasies. Although we have the ability to manifest whatever our heart desires, if they are not in harmony with eternity, we will ultimately manifest that which works against us. Manifesting faith however, involves bringing about the 'image' or vision that God has already planted in your heart, which ultimately works towards your good and more importantly, the good of others. Whether that vision requires you to become an Oscar award-winning actor, the President of the United States, the owner of a multi-billion dollar media company, or the genius behind the next big technological revolution.

Therefore, manifesting your God-given vision is about discovering your 'true passion' and in turn, being true to your self. It comes with the understanding that:

HIS PLAN IS YOUR PLAN.
YOUR DREAM IS HIS DREAM.
YOUR VISION IS HIS VISION.

Let there be light

The discovery of your God-given vision is key to releasing your potential. However, there is no vision without there first being light. In the Genesis account of creation, the command 'let there be light' was the very thing that set in motion the manifestation of the universe. As previously mentioned, the nature of light is to cause you to see, and give you vision. Discovering and manifesting your dream starts with seeing what God wants you to see. In order for that to happen, each of us must experience what I call a 'let there be light' moment. A 'let there be light' moment can come in the form of a revelation, an epiphany, an encounter, a visitation or any other 'eye-opening' experience. Unfortunately, sometimes we need to go through painful experiences in order to have our eyes opened. Experiences such as a divorce or a break up, loosing a job, a house, or even a friend can ultimately lead to you seeing opportunities that you would have otherwise ignored. In other cases, an eye-opening experience could simply be a matter of connecting with the right person. Whatever the case, we all need a 'let there be light' moment and most likely, several of them, in order to guide us on the path to destiny.

Principle Points:

1. Your passion is the greatest single clue
   to your true identity.

2. Daydreaming allows you to step out
   of your present reality and 'hang-out' in
   your future. It is key to bringing about the
   deepest desires of your heart.

3. Manifesting you God-given vision comes
   with the understanding that:
   YOUR VISION IS HIS VISION.

4. When you seek to fulfilll your God-given
   vision, everything will work together for
   your good.

5. You must give yourself permission to take
   the limits off yourself, and what you can
   achieve.

6. Discovering and manifesting your dream
   starts with seeing what God wants you to
   see.

7. Sometimes we need to go through painful
   experiences in order to have our eyes
   opened.

VISION

Chapter 11

USE TIME WELL

*God called the light Day, and the darkness
He called Night. So the evening and the
morning were the first day....*

"Then God said, "Let there be light"; and there was light. And God saw the light that it was good; and God divided the light from the darkness. God called the light Day, and the darkness He called Night. So the evening and the morning were the first day." (Genesis 1:3-5)

When light burst into the universe, creating the first day, time was born. There is nothing more powerful and significant than time! Time brings order to the universe. It frames and defines our physical world. Time is the medium by which thought becomes matter. It is the medium by which vision becomes a physical reality. Time is the magnetic component of your goals and desires.

In the Genesis account of creation, the universe was manifested in six days. The traditional understanding of this is that these six individual days served as intervals in which specific creative acts were carried out. For example, the land, seas and vegetation were manifested on the third day. This was followed by the manifestation of the sun, moon, and stars on the fourth day. However, what must be understood is that it was the **process** of time (as time passed from evening to morning) that brought about the manifestation. In other words, time itself is the active component of manifestation. If I were making a cake, I would first get the ingredients together. I would then arrange those ingredients into the form I wanted it to be in. Then in order for it to be complete, I would put it in the oven to bake. If I took the cake out of the oven *immediately* after I put it in, the cake would remain unfinished. The result would be the same no matter how high the temperature of the oven was. The only way the cake can be finished is by leaving it to bake over a period of time. In like manner, God calls forth the *ingredients*, such as the stars, moon, and sun, arranges them according to a set purpose then allows 'time' to complete the process. We see this in Genesis 1, where a period of time [evening to morning] followed each of God's creative commands.

Then God said, "Let there be light"; and there was light. And God saw the light, that it was good; and God divided the light from the darkness. God called the light Day, and the darkness He called Night. **So the evening and the morning were the first day**. Then God said, "Let there be a firmament in the midst of the waters, and let it divide the waters from the waters." Thus God made the firmament, and divided the waters which were under the firmament from the waters which were above the firmament; and it was so. And God called the firmament Heaven. **So the evening and the morning were the second day**. And God called the dry land Earth, and the gathering together of the waters He called Seas. And God saw that it was good. Then God said, "Let the earth bring forth grass, the herb that yields seed, and the fruit tree that yields fruit according to its kind, whose seed is in itself, on the earth"; and it was so. And the earth brought forth grass, the herb that yields seed according to its kind, and the tree that yields fruit, whose seed is in itself according to its kind. And God saw that it was good. **So the evening and the morning were the third day.**
(Genesis 1:6-13)

This was the method God used for everything He created. The six creative days mentioned served as the medium for bringing the world into existence. Nothing can be made without the aid and process of time. Time is attached to everything we do and everything we plan to do.

To everything there is a season, A time for every purpose under heaven: A time to be born, And a time to die; A time to plant, And a time to pluck what is planted; A time to kill, And a time

to heal; A time to break down, And a time to build up; A time to weep, And a time to laugh; A time to mourn, And a time to dance; A time to cast away stones, And a time to gather stones; A time to embrace, And a time to refrain from embracing; A time to gain, And a time to lose; A time to keep, And a time to throw away; A time to tear, And a time to sew; A time to keep silence, And a time to speak; A time to love, And a time to hate; A time of war, And a time of peace. (Ecclesiastes 3:8)

Long Time Perspective

Time, therefore, is a *creative force*. The most powerful tool a visionary can use. To that effect, plans and goals must become your key activity. When you set goals and make plans, you give time an assignment. Time correctly assigned or appointed will ensure that everything works toward the fulfilllment of your goals and vision. **Think of time as an unlimited amount of power that becomes more and more powerful in the future than in the present.** Therefore, in order to enhance the power of time, you must plan far into the future. The further your future plans, the more 'time-power' you allocate for yourself. Short-term plans yield lesser results. This fundamental truth was discovered and documented by Dr. Edward Banfield of Howard University. Banfield was a political scientist who made it his goal to find out how and why some people became financially independent during the course of their working lifetimes. He started off convinced that the answer to this question would be found in factors such as family background, education, intelligence, influential contacts, or some other concrete factor. What he finally discovered was that the major reason for success in life was a particular attitude towards time. Banfield called this attitude "long time perspective." Time perspective referred to how far you projected into the future when you decided what you were going to do or not do in the present. He said that men and women who were the most successful in life and the most likely to move up economically were those who took the future into consideration with every decision they made in the present. He described this as the most profound of all the principles for success.

The Power of Time

Arguably, the most profound example of the long time perspective is an event that should have led to Jesus' early demise. The book of Luke gives an account of a time when Jesus was teaching in the synagogue. There came a point when He said something that struck a nerve with those who were listening. Upon hearing this they became furious and mobbed Him and forced Him to the edge of a cliff in order to throw Him off. But He simply *passed right through the crowd and went on his way'* (Luke 4: 24-30 NLT). How was Jesus able to just pass right through a crowd so incensed on killing him? There is no record of either man or angels coming to his aid, nor did He have to fight in order to avoid an untimely death. The answer lies in the account given of other times where people tried to apprehend Him on account of the things He said:

"Then the leaders tried to arrest him; but no one laid a hand on him, because his time had not yet come." (John 7:30 NLT)

Jesus made these statements while he was teaching in the section of the Temple known as the Treasury. But he was not arrested, because **his time had not yet come.**

God is the ultimate when it comes to long-time perspective planning. The death of Jesus was meticulously planned and ordained long before His physical birth. When did this planning take place? According to the scriptures *"He was slain from the foundation of the world"* (Revelation 13:8). Wow! Bearing in mind Big Bang theorist estimate the universe to be over 13 billion years old, imagine the vast amount of time-power Jesus had working on His behalf. So much so, that when the angry crowd tried to throw Jesus off a cliff 'time' intervened! No one could take His life before the moment it was supposed to be taken. The same thing can happen for you when you adopt the same attitude towards time. Respect time and it will protect you, regardless of how imminent the situation is against you.

FOOD FOR THOUGHT

"The long term comes soon enough, and every sacrifice that you make today will be rewarded with compound interest in the great future that lies ahead for you."
- Brian Tracy

The Circle of Time

There is one more aspect of time that is so profound it takes a paradigm shift to truly understand it. Time is a circle! Although we experience time linearly, the truth is that we move and progress in circles. Everything about the universe is circular; whether it is the shape and motion of planets, or the same seasons we experience year after year. We live in a universe framed by repetition, patterns and cycles. If time is circular, then life is also circular. **Circles are where beginnings and endings meet at the same place.** What you must therefore understand is that in life, beginnings are in endings, and endings are in beginnings. The beginning must start from the end, and the beginning marks the end. This is the basic principle and paradigm of creation.

Achievement, therefore, is only possible when something

ends. Whether it is a job, a relationship, a way of living, or even a way of thinking, something must end in order for something to be achieved. Your dream, goals, or desired future will only come alive when something else dies. Don't be surprised when life becomes more turbulent when you set out to achieve your life's ambition. It is merely time bringing you to an end, in order for you to begin. In so doing, you will experience a whole series of beginnings and endings. If the turbulence is too much for you, then abandon your vision! Your vision will be the main reason for many of the demises in your life.

With the help of time, it will determine what will be kept or swept. That is why it is critical that you do not make any life long plans or decisions until you are clear about what you want to achieve. That way you will avoid making long term commitments to that which will be swept, and short term commitments to that which should be kept.

Principle Points:

1. Time is the medium by which thought becomes matter and vision becomes a physical reality.

2. Time is a creative force.

3. Time correctly assigned or appointed will ensure that everything works toward the fulfilllment of your goals and vision.

4. The most successful people in life are those who take the future into consideration with every decision they make in the present.

5. Time is a circle! Circles are where beginnings and endings meet at the same place.

6. Your dream, goals, or desired future will only come alive when something ends.

7. Respect time and it will protect you, regardless of how imminent the situation is against you.

Chapter 12

START FROM THE END

*I am the Alpha and the Omega,
the Beginning and the End...*

In the previous chapter, I touched on the fact that a visionary must project his or her plans far into the future in order to yield greater results. However, this does not mean you have to wait long before *'things happen.'* Your future plans can yield amazing results, just when you need it in the **here and now.** This can be best understood by examining the principles embedded in the scripture below:

"I am the Alpha and the Omega, the Beginning and the End," says the Lord, "who is and who was and who is to come, the Almighty." (Revelations 1:8)

In this profound statement the concept, nature, shape and power of time finds its conclusion in one indelible truth – **God is the very definition of time**. Hence the reason why I say there is nothing more powerful and significant than time. The Alpha [Beginning] and Omega [End] is the very reason why time is a circle. As explained in the previous chapter, the circle of time is composed of beginnings and endings existing in the same place. Where is this place? The answer can be found in the two words that precedes Alpha and Omega - I AM. Not only are the words I AM the most powerful words in the English dictionary, but grammatically speaking, every word or phrase immediately following I AM becomes *present tense*. So when God says, "I am the Alpha and the Omega, the Beginning and the End," He is saying that the beginning and the end exist in the here and now! Alpha and Omega are one and the same. As a result from a spiritual dimension, past, present and future are but a single event.

The Omega Principle

If indeed the beginning and end exist in the present, why start from the beginning when you can just be in the end? Earlier in this book, I mentioned the importance of daydreaming. Daydreaming allows you to step out of your present reality and 'hang-out' in your future. Taking this a step further, hanging out in your future is another key to manifesting your vision into physical reality. As Jack Canfield says, "When you visualize your goal, you give it a dynamic power that sets the stage for success." The dynamism of this power stems from our beliefs. The more of the future the mind experiences, the more dynamic the power to materialize your future in the present. This is what I call the *Omega principle*. The Omega principle is a powerful principle entirely focused on materializing your vision. To aid in the manifestation of our vision we must engage ourselves in **end-time activities**. In using the term 'end-time' I am not referring to the apocalypse or anything so dramatic! I am instead referring to the end of your goal, vision, or desired outcome. Let us say for example that your goal is to become an Oscar award-winning actor. You can exercise the Omega principle by imagining yourself playing the type of role that other actors who have won Oscars are known for.

Imagine the dramatic scenes you played that in your opinion 'clinched the deal.'

Imagine the feeling of hearing your name announced as one of the nominees.

Imagine yourself as a nominee seated in the Kodak Theatre with the likes of Will Smith, Meryl Streep, Denzel Washington, or Daniel Day Lewis. Imagine the exhilaration of hearing your name called out by last year's Oscar award winner.

Imagine the applause and the pat on the shoulder as you kiss your spouse and leave your seat to collect your prize. Imagine the teary-eyed acceptance speech you give as you cling hold of that weighty gold statuette.

These are but a few examples of end-time activities you must engage in order to exercise the Omega principle. But, it is not enough to just imagine, there are practical things you must also do. Such as,

- Write an acceptance speech and reading it to yourself daily
- Have someone giving you a post Oscar Awards interview
- Emulate the thoughts of Oscar Award Winning Actors. Read or watch their interviews. Find out how they think, what makes them tick, and commonalities they all share.
- Study the techniques and preparation

methods of other award winning Actors and practicing them for the leading role you've just booked (imaginary or otherwise).

These are but a few examples of end-time activities that could be deployed to exercise the Omega principle. The good thing is that nothing is preventing you from engaging in your end-time activities right now. By so doing, you are changing your reality, first from the inside, until it eventually manifests externally. **The more 'believable' your activities, the more real it will become.**

When you start from the end, things start to happen. This is because your commitment to you future brings power to you present. Operating the Omega principle initiates the Alpha (beginning) in your life. Ultimately, it is the 'effect' that brings about the 'cause.'

---FOOD FOR THOUGHT---

"Embody your dreams and you'll attract what you need to bring them to life."
- Jack Canfield

Therefore, set your mind on the end in order to bring about the beginning. Never begin a project or enterprise without first visualizing and preparing for the end result. If you desire to be an author, here's a question: do you want to be an author or an author that sells books? The main reason why many authors gain very little sales from their book is because they have no plan or strategy in place beyond the completion of their book. If your goal was just to write a book, then your point of relief will be set at the completion of your book. However, if you want to sell copies of your book, then your point of relief must go well beyond writing your book. The same principle applies to anything else you want to achieve, start from the end in order to begin.

Principle Points:

1. God is the very definition of time.
   He is the point where time begins
   and ends

2. God is the Alpha and Omega. Therefore,
   the beginning and the end exist in
   the here and now!

3. If indeed the beginning and end exist in
   the present, the instead of starting from
   the beginning you can just be in the end.

4. The more of the future your mind
   experiences, the more dynamic the
   power to materialize your future in
   the present.

5. To aid in the manifestation of our vision
   you must engage yourself in end-time
   activities.

6. Never begin a project or enterprise
   without first visualizing and preparing for
   the end result.

7. Embody your dreams and you'll attract
   what you need to bring them to life.
   - Jack Canfield

VISION

PART THREE

THE POWER OF VISION

INTRO

What you see through the eyes of your imagination is key to the releasing of your creative power. As previously mentioned, we are creatures that function by images and imagination. Our whole world is swayed by how we handle, process, and manifest images. We were purposely created that way so that we can wield the power of faith. The power of faith is in essence the power of vision. It works according to your response to your inner vision. When you act according to your inner vision, nothing can stop you from turning your dream into a physical reality.

Chapter 13

SEE, BELIEVE, TAKE ACTION AND RECEIVE

If only I may touch His clothes, I shall be made well...

What you see through the eyes of your imagination is key to the releasing of your creative power. As previously mentioned, we are creatures that function by *images and imagination*. Our whole world is swayed by how we handle, process and manifest images. We were purposely created that way so that we can wield the power of vision. The power of vision is in essence the power of faith. It works according to your *response to your inner vision*. **When you** 'act' according to your inner vision, you release the **power of faith.** Action confirms your belief in your vision. The famed woman with the issue of blood received her healing because she acted upon what she saw in her heart.

Now a certain woman had a flow of blood for twelve years, and had suffered many things from many physicians. She had spent all that she had and was no better, but rather grew worse. When she heard about Jesus, she came behind Him in the crowd and touched His garment. For she said, "If only I may touch His clothes, I shall be made well." Immediately the fountain of her blood was dried up, and she felt in her body that she was healed of the affliction. And Jesus, immediately knowing in Himself that power had gone out of Him, turned around in the crowd and said, "Who touched My clothes?" But His disciples said to Him, "You see the multitude thronging You, and You say, Who touched Me?" And He looked around to see her who had done this thing. But the woman, fearing and trembling, knowing what had happened to her, came and fell down before Him and told Him the whole truth. And He said to her, "Daughter, your faith has made you well. Go in peace, and be healed of your affliction." (Mark 5:25-34)

This woman suffered from a condition that was so chronic that she constantly hemorrhaged for some twelve years. However,

>**despite** the stigma of an embarrassing disease,
>**despite** being deemed unclean and therefore
>barred from the synagogue and public places,
>**despite** the humiliation of having been

exposed and subjected to the primitive
practice of many male physicians,
despite the disappointment of having
undergone all sorts of medical treatments
that only served to make her condition worse,
despite being devastated physically,
financially and emotionally,
despite the pain of loneliness and rejection,
despite the hostility of her society and environment,

She went into the crowd, pressing pass people she knew, people who despised her, people who felt she had no right to be there. With unfettered focus and relentlessness she grasped the hem of Jesus garment and her flow of blood ceased. The way this woman received her healing was totally unprecedented. Never before in the annals of the scriptures, had anyone received healing *without* a man of God's knowledge or consent. Never before also, had anyone received their healing **on-purpose** and by their own actions. So how did she receive her healing without direct action from Jesus? First of all, she made the following declaration, "if only I may touch His clothes, I shall be made well." As mentioned earlier, words are in essence images. It is impossible to speak or think without materializing a corresponding image or vision. Therefore, in saying what she said, a mental picture of her touching Jesus' clothes and being healed would have automatically appeared in her mind. She believed in what she saw, which was evidenced by the action of pushing through the crowd to touch Jesus. She was therefore healed because she:

SAW, BELIEVED, TOOK ACTION and RECEIVED.

She imagined herself being healed just by touching the clothes He was wearing. Indeed that is what happened when she acted accordingly. I can imagine that with each step she took, the vision got clearer and brighter, which in turn made her more determined and courageous. With each step her faith would have grown stronger and stronger, culminating in divine through the power of vision. Like this woman, your power emanates from acting on what you can see in the depths of your imagination. **When you see it you can achieve it.** This is the power of vision. When you harness the power of vision, nothing you imagine to do will be impossible for you. Your vision is the key to:

- Overcoming the insurmountable,
- Solving the insuperable,
- Defeating the invincible,
- and achieving the impossible.

All you have to do is see, believe, take action and receive.

Principle Points:

1. The power of vision is in essence the power of faith. It works according to your response to your inner vision.

2. When you see it you can achieve it.

3. When you harness the power of vision, nothing you imagine to do will be impossible for you.

4. The woman with the issue of blood received her healing because she SAW, BELIEVED, TOOK ACTION and RECEIVED.

5. Action confirms your belief in your vision.

Chapter 14

BE INSPIRED

*Whatever the Father does, the Son also does in
like manner...*

Inspiration is the process of being motivated or mentally stimulated to achieve something. When you are inspired you are more likely to achieve your goals. To quote John Maxwell,

"People are not lazy. They simply have impotent goals – that is, goals that do not inspire them."

Although inspiration comes in many forms, you are most 'inspired' when you are motivated to do exactly what you see someone else doing. Bruce Lee is widely considered to be the greatest and most influential martial artists of all time. His superior fighting skills and agility was the inspiration behind a host of highly skilled martial artists who saw themselves doing what Bruce was doing. Many of us are inspired in the same way when we see our 'heroes' in action. Whether it is our parents, mentors, community leaders, athletes, or the like. Even fictitious characters like Batman, Superman or Wonder Woman can be a source of inspiration to us! No matter how great or incredible the person, we are inspired when we see ourselves doing exactly what we see our heroes or mentors do.

You can do it

Inspiration is an essential part of fulfilling one's vision. This is because it ignites your passion and releases your creative power, which we now understand to be wisdom. It is no wonder why ancient Greeks believed that inspiration was a gift from the gods! Your creative power is released because inspiration carries a letter addressed only for your heart. This letter contains four simple words that make a powerful impact. Those words are 'YOU CAN DO IT.' When these four words are sown deep in the soil of your heart, there is nothing you cannot achieve. The last word (it) in this powerful statement represents your dream, your passion, your assignment, and your purpose. In a nutshell, it represents your vision. 'You can do it' therefore empowers you to achieve what you can see. The more you believe you can do it, the more you will achieve what you see. That is why it is good to be self-motivated. Simply put, self-motivation is your own ability to sow the message of 'you can do it' in your own heart. People who are self-motivated can find a reason and strength to complete a task, even throughout challenging situations.

Divine Inspiration

Although it is good to be self-motivation, you are more likely to believe 'you can do it' when you are divinely inspired. Divine inspiration comes in the form of a vision of what you can achieve. Divine inspiration gives you assurance of the highest level of authority, permission, and approval. Divine inspiration gives you the following:

- The Vision of what you can achieve
- The Message that you can achieve it
- The Authority to achieve it
- The Power to achieve it

Your vision is more than a wish or intention. It is the endorsement of your creative power and the authority to achieve what you see. This fact leads us to the profound truth behind all supernatural things Jesus was able to achieve...

Principle Points:

1. You are most 'inspired' when you are motivated to do exactly what you see someone else doing.

2. Inspiration empowers you to achieve what you see.

3. Inspiration carries a letter addressed only for your heart. This letter contains four simple words that make a powerful impact: 'YOU CAN DO IT.'

4. You are more likely to believe 'you can do it' when you are divinely inspired.

5. Divine inspiration gives you assurance of the highest level of authority, permission, and approval.

6. Your vision is more than a wish or intention. It is the endorsement of your creative power and the authority to achieve what you see.

Chapter 15

THE DIVINE POWER OF VISION

*The Son can do nothing of Himself, but
what He sees the Father do...*

Divine inspiration was the key to all the supernatural things Jesus performed. As previously explained, you are inspired when you are motivated to do exactly what you see your heroes or mentors doing. This in turn activates your creative power. In principle, this is what happened when Jesus saw what His Father did.

Then Jesus answered and said to them, "Most assuredly, I say to you, the Son can do nothing of Himself, but what He sees the Father do; for whatever He does, the Son also does in like manner." (John 5:19)

All the miraculous things He did stemmed from what He saw His Father doing in Heaven. His ability to see the Father was not by divine visitation but by what was revealed in the imagination of His heart. What He saw in His heart gave Him the inspiration, endorsement, approval, and authorization required to fulfilll His vision. He could not do anything He did not see His Father doing. This illustrates the significance, influence, and power of vision.

Seeing the Father

As mentioned, vision was the key to all the supernatural things Jesus achieved. As intriguing as this is, how does this relate to ordinary folk like you and me? After all, the Bible makes it clear that no one has seen the Father, except His Son, Jesus. That being the case, how is it possible for us to harness the divine power of vision if we cannot see the Father? To answer this question, we need to understand what it really is to see the Father. Firstly, when Jesus said He only does what He sees His Father doing, whom did He really see? I pose this question because when Philip asked

Jesus to reveal the Father Jesus gave the following response:

Jesus said to him, "Have I been with you so long, and yet you have not known Me, Philip? He who has seen Me has seen the Father; so how can you say, 'Show us the Father'?"
(John 14:7-9)

Jesus is the express image of the Father. Seeing Him is seeing the Father. Therefore, when Jesus said, "I only do what I see the Father doing" the person He saw was Himself! However, in seeing Himself, He understood that He was really seeing the Father. **If you were Jesus**, all your achievements would be based on your heavenly Father, giving you a vision of 'you' doing something great. However, the image of 'you' in the vision is in effect, Him [Totally profound!]. The good thing is that 'in Christ' **you are Jesus**. According to the scriptures when you accept Jesus into your life, His life literally becomes your life.

"If then you were raised with Christ, seek those things which are above, where Christ is, sitting at the right hand of God. Set your mind on things above, not on things on the earth. **For you died, and your life is hidden with Christ in God. When Christ who is our life** appears, then you also will appear with Him in glory." (Colossians 3:1-4)

From Heaven's perspective, you become a new creature when you accept Christ. The 'old you' has passed away and Christ is now your life. When Christ is your life, you are one with Him. That being the case, whatever applies to Christ Jesus also applies to you. If Christ is the image and face of the Father, then so are you. As a result, when God gives you a vision of 'you' doing something great, the 'you' in the vision is in effect, Him! That is why you should never be afraid of your 'big vision,' where you see yourself achieving something far beyond your present scope and resources. It is big because it is what God will accomplish through you.

Therefore, as a visionary , you are a tool in the hands of The Creator. You are His chisel, paintbrush, scalpel, and pen. You are His solution for the pain of your community. You are the sword by which He will vanquish the enemies of peace. You are the vessel He will use to usher in a brighter future.

Principle Points:

1. Divine inspiration was the key to all the supernatural things Jesus performed.

2. All the miraculous things He did stemmed from what He saw His Father doing in Heaven. This was revealed in the imagination of His heart.

3. Jesus is the express image of the Father. Seeing Him is seeing the Father.

4. If you were Jesus, all your achievements would stem from your heavenly Father, giving you a vision of 'you' doing great things However the image of 'you' in the vision is in effect, Him.

5. In Christ you are Jesus. As a result, when God gives you a vision of 'you' doing something great, the 'you' in the vision is in effect, Him!

6. Never be afraid of your 'big dream.' It is big, because it is what God will accomplish through you.

7. God dwells in the imagination of His visionaries.

---

*God dwells in the imagination
of His visionaries.*

Choose Christ

To choose Christ is to choose life.
Not an ordinary life but a rich trichotomy of purpose,
power, and destiny. It is life at the highest level of living
brought about by the highest level of thinking. It is
life where dire circumstances can be changed and not
just accepted. A life where impossibilities are merely the
product of unbelief and possibilities are subject to what we
choose to believe.

To Choose Christ is to choose dominion.
You were created to have dominion on the earth. That
means you are supposed to have dominion over anything
that challenges your wellbeing and the wellbeing of others.
Whether it is in the area of your finances, health, career,
relationships, or spiritual growth, in Christ you have
dominion over them all.

When you choose Christ,
you choose to stand boldly and shine in your uniqueness,
rather than sit on the bench of commonality.
Your uniqueness is the solution to the needs of a specific
set of people. Your uniqueness is linked to the gifts and

talents that God meticulously wove into your divine make up. Your gifts and talents are what make you unique.

We were all created
with particular gifts and talents.
Some are discovered early in life and others later. Often times we either sit on our talents or put them to improper use. Only a few are fortunate enough to make a global impact with their gift and fewer still manage to find the true purpose of their gift. In Christ, God uses your gifts, talents and ultimately your uniqueness to bring you to your place of influence. In your place of influence you are strategically positioned to positively impact the world or to prevent the outcome of a dire situation.

That is your purpose.
That is your destiny.

The world is waiting for your divine light to shine!
This can only be achieved in Christ, where you discover your 'true self.' You are a goldmine and only 'The One' you knows you better than yourself, can help you mine the 'abundant treasure' buried within you.

www.ingramcontent.com/pod-product-compliance
Lightning Source LLC
Chambersburg PA
CBHW071830190726
48292CB00005B/1700